A B C D E

F G H I J

K L M N

O P Q R S

T U V W

X Y Z

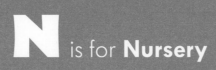

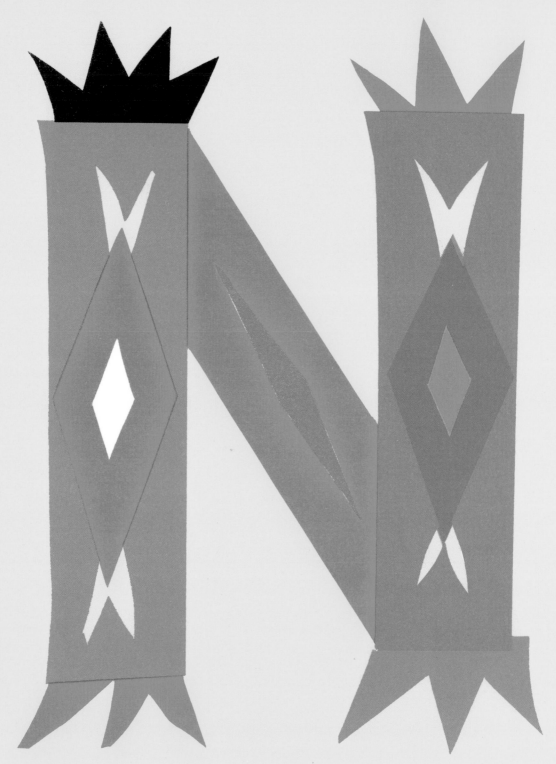

For Florence Schulman

IS FOR NURSERY

by **Blossom Budney**
Illustrated by **Vladimir Bobri**

In my nursery school, we have our teacher,
And the girls, and the boys, so
A is for all of us — everyone,
Playing, learning, having fun.

We **build** in school with **big** wood **blocks**,
Then stack them **back** inside their **box**.
But **birthdays** are the best of Bs.
We've special treats on days with these.
(Let the birthday child blow out the candles, please.)

Chairs in a **circle** — for stories and songs.
Cupboards — to keep each thing where it belongs.
C for crayons, clay and chalk;
For clean-up-time at twelve o'clock.

We've **dolls**, we've **dishes**, we play **dress-up**.
And each of us has a **drinking** cup.
D for this picture that I **drew**.
D for 'don't', and D for 'do'.

E for our ears, and E for our eyes —
Using them will make us wise.
Some days we take a trip — exploring.
(Once when we did it started pouring!)

F for fingers — five on each hand
To finger paint, to write with, and
For patting, pointing, and sifting sand.
F for our friends, and F for the fun
Inside our school and in the sun.

G for good-morning — that starts the day.

G for all the games we play.

G for giggling — that's silly fun.

G for good-bye when school is done.

H for hands, they can hit or hold,
Or busily shake, or quietly fold.

I is for important. I am — and you —
And people, and places, and things that we do.
I for an idea, written or said,
Or just a thought popping into your head.

J is for jumping up and down.
J is for jolly, like our puppet clown.
J is juice-time at half past ten;
Then after juice, we play again.

K is for kindness to each other;
For kissing our friends, and dad, and mother.

In our school, things are little and low —
Just the right height for us, you know.
We can reach what we need, and we fit where we sit,
And our schoolroom is sunny and cheerfully lit.

M is for music — we're all fine singers.

M is for mittens, to warm our fingers.

M's for my mother, and also for me.

I take home what I make, for my mother to see.

N for naughty, N for nice,
For **never needing** to be called twice.

O is for overalls most of us wear,
And left and right oxfords — two shoes to a pair.
O for the 'ouch!' we can't help saying
If we get bumped while we are playing.

P for politeness, for saying 'please'.
For pictures, and our pets — all these.

Q. Sometimes it's quiet. (That's when we rest.)
Then just before noon we quickly get dressed.

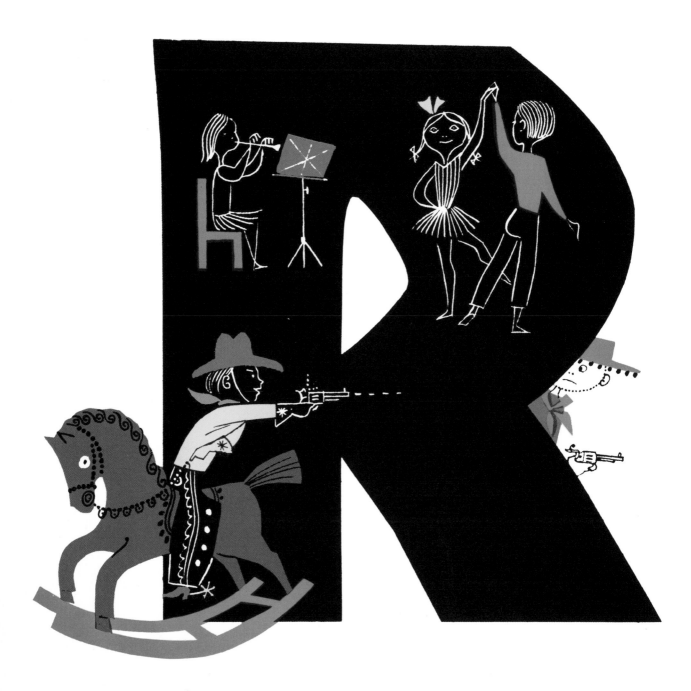

R for our rubbers, R for the rain
Rapping and tapping against the pane.
Rhythms. This R means music and dancing.
R for our rocking horse, riding and prancing.

S is silly words we love to say.
And smiling, in a pleasant way.
In school, we all learn how to share.
(That's one way of being fair).

Taking turns is another way.

T for together, the way that we play.

T for telling about what we do;

For toes, for ten, for tickling, too.

Our teacher never gets upset.
Whatever we do, she doesn't fret.
She understands (it starts with U)
All the things that we need to do.

V for getting **vaccinations**,
For visitors, and for vacations.
V for our voices. We do make noise!
But then we are fifteen girls and boys!

W. Our questions start this **way** —
Who? Where? Why? What did you say?

Our nursery school has no **xylophone**,
So we have no X's of our own.

Y is for yes, for yelling, for you,
And Y for yippee! and yesterday, too.

It's not in our school, but a trip we took
Will make two Z's to go in my book.
A school bus drove us one day to the zoo.
And guess what we saw? ...... A zebra. You knew!

EXIT

The Bodleian Library is home to the Iona and Peter Opie Collection
of Children's Books, one of the largest and most important collections of
children's books in the English language.

Published in 2017 by the Bodleian Library
Broad Street, Oxford OX1 3BG

www.bodleianshop.co.uk

ISBN: 978 1 85124 482 9

Designed and typeset in 20/25pt Monotype Twentieth Century by Dot Little in the
Bodleian Library
Printed and bound by Toppan, China on 150gsm Senbo Munk Dkal FSC paper

British Library Catalogue in Publishing Data
A CIP record of this publication is available from the British Library